Arctic Adventures

Short Stories, Fuzzy Animals and Life Lessons

Karma for Kids Books

Norma MacDonald

Arctic Adventures
Short Stories, Fuzzy Animals and Life Lessons

Copyright © 2018 Norma MacDonald

First Edition

Published by: Find Your Way Publishing, Inc.
PO BOX 667
Norway, ME 04268 U.S.A.
www.findyourwaypublishing.com

ISBN-13: 978-1-945290-14-5

ISBN-10: 1-945290-14-5

Library of Congress Control Number: 2018936053

Printed in the United States of America.

Dedication

This book is dedicated to all the people trying to make the world a better place. You are making a positive difference!

"If you want to lift yourself up,
lift up someone else."
~ Booker T. Washington

Table of Contents

About This Book

Welcome to our Karma for Kids Book Series. We are grateful that you picked up this book. We believe together we can make a positive difference, one child at a time. We strive to instill important life lessons in the lives of young children. We are firm believers that we reap what we sow and think that if this simple lesson is taught to children at a young age, their lives have the potential to be absolutely amazing.

We once knew a dog named Karma. She was a beautiful Labrador retriever. It wasn't until after she passed, at 11 years old, that we realized just how fitting her name really was.

Karma is indeed a retriever.

Whatever we threw out, Karma was always happy to bring it back to us. It didn't matter what it was, she always brought it back. If we threw out an ugly, stinky, dirty sock she'd bring it back without question. If we threw out a sweet smelling, beautiful bouquet of flowers she'd bring it back. It's the same in life. Whatever you send out, is what you will get back, guaranteed, every time. Our Karma for Kids Book Series hopes to instill this easy-to-understand lesson into the lives of children at a young age. The Universe wants to happily bring you all that your heart desires, and it will, effortlessly. But first, you've got to throw out what you want it to bring back to you so that it can! Have fun with this and watch the magic happen. God bless!

Find all of Norma MacDonald's Karma for Kids Books at Amazon.com.

For more of our Karma for Kids books please visit us at:

www.karmaforkidsbooks.wordpress.com
or
www.findyourwaypublishing.com

Other books that we recommend to help children learn important life lessons:

Kyle Kitten and Friends: Short Stories, Fuzzy Animals, and Life Lessons by Norma MacDonald

Other books continued:

The Panda Family Relies on Each Other: Short Stories, Fuzzy Animals, and Life Lessons by Norma MacDonald
Matt the African Meerkat and Friends: Short Stories, Fuzzy Animals, and Life Lessons by Norma MacDonald

Kimmie Koala and Friends: Short Stories, Fuzzy Animals, and Life Lessons by Norma MacDonald

Cranky Crocodile Saves the Day: Short Stories, Fuzzy Animals, and Life Lessons by Norma MacDonald

The Many Adventures of Peppy the Emperor Penguin: Short Stories, Fuzzy Animals, and Life Lessons by Norma MacDonald

Lucy Llama and Friends: Short Stories, Fuzzy Animals, and Life Lessons by Norma MacDonald

Ethan Eagle and Friends: Short Stories, Fuzzy Animals, and Life Lessons by Norma MacDonald

Billy Brown Bear and Friends: Short Stories, Fuzzy Animals, and Life Lessons by Norma MacDonald

Humble Heron and Friends: Short Stories, Fuzzy Animals, and Life Lessons by Norma MacDonald

Peter Penguin and Friends: Short Stories, Fuzzy Animals and Life Lessons by Norma MacDonald

Guaranteed Success for Kindergarten; 50 Easy Things You Can Do Today! by Marrae Kimball

Guaranteed Success for Grade School; 50 Easy Things You Can Do Today! by Marrae Kimball

The Secret Combination to Middle School: Real Advice from Real Kids, Ideas for Success, and Much More! by Marrae Kimball

Arctic Adventures

Short Stories, Fuzzy Animals, and Life Lessons

Karma for Kids Books

Norma MacDonald

Chapter One

The month of June brings bright and long days to the land at the top of the earth called the Arctic. During the summer months, the sun stays high in the sky both day and night. This unique area is the land of polar bears, caribou, puffins and many other amazing animals. Few people live in the Arctic. First Nation people who live in this frigid land are called the Inuit, which means "the people" in their native language.

The Inuit hunt and fish and use snowmobiles to move across the snowy frozen ground. They share the land with the animals, many of which are also hunters and fishers. Some of those animals are also hunted. Their lives are in constant danger. This is true of the arctic hare. So every year, the grown up hares organize competitions to encourage their young ones to run faster and jump higher--training that can save their lives.

Miki is a young arctic hare, also called a polar rabbit. In the winter it's easy for her to hide in the snow because her fur is bright white. During those cold months, Miki and the other rabbits stay warm by digging shelters in the snow and huddling together with friends and family. There isn't much to eat in winter.

Miki spends her days dreaming about all the food she will be able to enjoy when summer arrives. She also looks forward to becoming a champion. This is the year she plans to be the fastest runner and highest jumper of all. Miki likes to be the best at everything.

Last summer Miki came in second in the running and jumping competitions, but she knows that if she works really hard, she can win them all. She trains every day.

A week before the polar rabbits come out of their snowy dens, Miki decides it's time to work harder. She uses her front paws to do a hundred push-ups every morning and every night. Ten times a day she jumps up and down for fifteen minutes. Her brothers and sisters complain. "Miki keeps bumping into us and is shaking the entire den," they say. "We can't sleep."

Miki's parents sit Miki down for a talk. "Training is good for you, but you need to think of yourself and others," they say. "There is a time to train and a time to rest. You need to take more time to rest."

"But if I stop training, I won't get strong and I won't be able to win the competitions at the end of the summer," she cries.

"Winning is not the most important thing in life," her father says. "It is more important to have peace with your friends and family. And if you keep disturbing everyone in this den every day, they might just kick you out in the cold!"

Miki grumbles, but she has no choice but to obey her father. So, she still does quiet push-ups when everyone else is sleeping and does little jumps as often as she can get away with it.

It is an especially happy day for all the arctic animals when the weather warms. The rabbits can leave their snowy dens and many of the animals shed their heavy white fur coats and put on light summer ones. The rabbits jump and skip and fill their bellies full with the tender first green sprigs of grass that emerge from the melting snow. It won't be long until the bushes put out their buds and leaves. Miki's favorite time is when the berries ripen. Berries are so yummy!

Miki is especially happy to come out of the den because now she can run and jump and run and jump and no one can complain. First thing in the morning she wakes up and runs ten times around the meadow as fast as she can. Her back legs are very strong and powerful. In order to go faster, Miki imagines she's being chased by an arctic fox, one of the polar rabbit's most dangerous enemies.

"Why are you running so fast?" asks one of the baby rabbits as Miki whizzes by. "You're making me dizzy."

Miki doesn't stop to answer. She runs faster and faster. A crowd of baby rabbits gather to watch and cheer her on. Their clapping and shouting gives her even more energy, so she does an extra lap around the meadow. When she stops to rest, the group of baby rabbits gather around her.

"Why do you run and run and run?" they ask. "Are you scared of getting caught by a fox? Do you think we need to run and run and run, too?"

"I'm not afraid of foxes," Miki brags. "I'm the fastest rabbit in the Arctic. But all of you need to be careful."

"We promise." The baby rabbits agree. "You are for sure the fastest rabbit around."

Miki stretches out her legs and smiles with happiness. She is positive that she will win all the races and jumping competitions. No one else is training and preparing like she is.

As the big day of competition gets closer, Miki runs and jumps more and more. Sometimes her friends come by and invite her to play games together, but Miki just shakes her head as she huffs and puffs, "Too busy for games. Champions have no time to play."

"I sure am glad I'm not a champion," says one of Miki's friends. "I'd rather have fun and play."

Miki's parents also encourage her to take time to rest, but she doesn't listen to them either. "Champions have no time to rest," Miki says.

But Miki would be wise to listen to her parents.

The day before the competition, her mother notices that Miki is very hot. She has a fever. "But I don't feel sick," Miki says. She tries to convince her mother that she can still go out for her morning run.

"Absolutely not, my dear daughter," she says. "You need to go straight to bed."

Miki bursts into tears, "But if I don't train today, I won't win tomorrow!"

Her mother pats her gently on the shoulder. "You won't be competing tomorrow."

"But I have to run tomorrow," Miki cries. "I have to be the champion."

"If you don't rest, you will get sicker. Winning isn't everything, Miki. And there's always next year."

Miki's shoulders droop and her heart sinks as she curls up into a ball to sleep. The fever gives her wild dreams. She imagines she is being chased by giant white foxes with long, yellow teeth. She wakes up in the morning wet with sweat. Her mother is beside her. "How do you feel this morning, little one?"

Miki stretches her legs. She feels weak and tired and thirsty. "I guess I won't be able to race today," she says, her eyes welling with tears.

Her mother nods. "Next year. I understand you're disappointed, but you and your health are more important."

Miki frowns. "Next year I will train, but I will make sure I have time out to rest and play with my friends, too."

Her mother hugs her. "I've very proud of you, Miki. Patience and balance are very important lessons to learn. You've got this. Now, let's get you rested and feeling better."

Chapter Two

Many miles north of the dens of the arctic rabbits, polar bears roam the frozen land in constant search of something to eat. Polar bears are large and powerful and need to eat a huge amount of food. The harp seal is their favorite meal, but the seals are very hard to catch. The polar bears sometimes wait many hours for the seals to come to the top of the sea ice to breathe. That takes a lot of patience. Sometimes they don't have to kill their food. Once in a while, a big whale dies and the polar bears can eat it. The polar bears have great noses and can smell a dead whale from twenty miles away. That's far!

As the sun comes up over the eastern sky, two young polar bears roam over the thick ice in search of food. Their tummies grumble because they haven't found anything to eat for a whole week. These two polar bears, Kallik and Muktuk, are twin brothers. Kallik thinks he knows everything. But Muktuk isn't like that. He is always willing to listen to his brother. They do everything together. But sometimes they get in arguments because Kallik doesn't listen to his brother. This makes their parents sad.

This day these brother bears are grouchy because they are hungry. Kallik wants to sit and wait for a seal at one of the holes in the sea ice, but Muktuk would rather keep walking. He thinks he smells a dead whale.

"You always think you smell a dead whale," says his brother. "How many times have we walked around and around and around and there's no dead whale? You've never found a whale."

Muktuk shakes his head. "And you never make mistakes, right?"

"My nose is never wrong," says Kallik in defense. "My nose always leads us to a dead whale. And I am telling you now." He sniffs the air. "There's no dead whale anywhere near here."

Muktuk sniffs the air again. "I smell a dead whale. I know I smell it. This time I am not imagining things."

Kallik shoves against his brother's shoulder. "If you think you're right, go! But I am staying right here. And I am going to eat a juicy, fat seal while you wander around the ice looking for a dead whale that doesn't exist. Then we'll know who's right and who's wrong. We will know who has the best nose. And that's me!"

Muktuk's heart feels sad. "I'm leaving now," he says and walks away from his brother.

Kallik shouts after him. "I will be sure to save a piece of meat for when you come back with an empty stomach."

Muktuk would rather stay with his brother and wait for a seal, but he is so hungry and he is sure that there is a dead whale nearby. It's true he has been wrong before, but this time is different. So he puts his nose in the air and follows the scent. The further he goes, the stronger the smell becomes.

In the meantime, Kallik waits at the ice hole. He waits and waits and waits. No seal comes to the hole to take a breath. His tummy hurts from hunger pains. He wishes his brother was there so they could tell stories to each other. That's how they usually pass the time. "Muktuk should have listened to me," he says to himself. "My nose is never wrong."

Muktuk has been walking for over an hour in the bright sun. He starts to have doubts. Maybe his brother was right. Maybe there's no dead whale after all. He thinks about turning around and going back to his brother. But the smell gets stronger. He narrows his eyes and peers into the distance, but all he sees is ice, ice, and more ice. His tummy grumbles and his mouth waters. He can almost taste the dead whale already. Plus he knows his entire family will be able to eat if he can just find that dead whale. So he keeps going.

At the ice hole, Kallik keeps waiting. Where are the harp seals? The polar bear twins had caught many seals at this very spot, but this week there has not been a single one. How much longer can they live without eating? Kallik scoops up a piece of ice and pops it in his mouth to get a drink of water. He wonders when Muktuk will give up and come back. It's been hours since he left. Maybe their parents have had more success hunting today. Kallik imagines how happy they would all be to finally sit down and stuff their tummies. "If Muktuk doesn't come back soon, I'm going home without him," Kallik says to himself.

Muktuk's feet hurt. He is tired of walking. The smell of the dead whale is stronger than ever, but he can't see anything. He has almost decided to give up and turn back when he spots a dark hump sticking out from the white ice. He rubs his eyes to make sure he's not seeing things. But the big dark lump is still there. Muktuk breaks out in a run and within five minutes, his eyes are filled with the body of a black and white orca which is also called a killer whale. Muktuk dances with glee and lets out a happy roar. His voice echoes across the ice.

The twin's parents, who are hunting about a mile away, hear Muktuk's voice and head towards him. When they arrive, he has already filled his belly. He is thrilled to see them. "Eat. Eat. Eat," he says.

"Where's your brother?" asks his mother.

Muktuk sighs. "He didn't believe I smelled a whale. He's waiting at an ice hole. I was just about to go get him." With that, Muktuk rushes off to find his brother.

Kallik sees Muktuk from a distance. "Finally," he says, and races off to meet him. When he gets close he shouts, "It took you long enough. So, you finally gave up on that imaginary whale smell?"

"You still hungry?" Muktuk shouts back with a huge grin on his face. He pats his belly. "I haven't eaten this much in months."

The twins meet and walk together. "You are joking?" says Kallik, unable to believe his brother actually found a dead whale.

"No joke," says Muktuk. "Follow me. Mother and father are already eating."

Kallik and Muktuk race each other to the place where Muktuk found the whale. Because Kallik hasn't eaten and is tired, he can't keep up with Muktuk, who has a full belly. Kallik mumbles and grumbles. He's not used to falling behind his brother.

When the twins arrive at the whale, their parents are relaxing and seem to be very grateful for their sons find. "Thank you, Muktuk. Your good nose may have saved our family from starvation," says his father.

Kallik is busy eating, but when he hears what his father says, he frowns. Kallik still can't believe that his brother smelled the whale and he didn't.

His mother draws close and sits down beside him. "What's wrong, Kallik? Aren't you happy that your brother found food for all of us?"

Kallik grunts.

His mother is wise and guesses what the problem is. "So, you think you should have been the one who found the whale and not your brother, right?"

"But I have a better nose," he said. "I am always the one who finds the whales."

"Are you jealous of your brother?" she asks. "Can't you be happy that he found his first whale? Maybe you should be open to listening to him more often. It is good to be happy for others."

"I'm not jealous," he says. But he is. That's why he didn't listen to him. His mother leaves him alone to think about what she said.

A little while later, Muktuk approaches his twin brother. "Did you get enough to eat?"

Kallik nods. Though it's hard for him, he takes a deep breath and gives thanks to his brother. "I'm glad your nose is working and that you found this whale. I'm sorry I didn't listen to you. This has helped me realize that I'm not always right. No one is."

Muktuk is both surprised and happy as he accepts his brother's apology. Maybe now his brother will listen to him more. He's excited for their next outing together.

Chapter Three

In the wintertime, when the sun comes out only for a few hours, it's hard to spot a family of arctic foxes. Their coats are snowy white, just like the ice and snow that surround them. For the birds, which are hunted by the foxes, this can be a real problem. Especially for the lemmings, which is the foxes favorite food.

When summer arrives and the Arctic is filled with sunshine, the foxes coats change from white to brown and yellow. This also makes them hard to spot, since they blend in with the grass and flowers of the meadows. When they crouch down, they become almost invisible.

Arctic foxes are wise hunters. Besides their usual food, they also search out bird's nests and try to get the eggs. But the easiest meals of all are when the foxes can eat what's left behind after a polar bear has finished a meal. Leftovers are the best!

Lusa is one of the greatest of the young hunters, because she doesn't give up easily. Even when everyone else in her family calls it quits for the day, she keeps up the hunt.

"Your head is as hard as a rock," her father often says. And it's true. Lusa is hard-headed. Stubborn. That means when she wants to do something, it is very, very hard to stop her. And it's super difficult to get her to do something when she doesn't want to do it. Sometimes this causes problems for her. But other times it's a good thing.

Lusa has a problem. She doesn't like to eat most birds. This is a big problem, since birds are the main thing that arctic foxes eat. Even when she's hungry, Lusa refuses to eat birds. "Birds are too bony and they taste yucky," she complains.

Once when she was little, she went a whole week without eating because she refused to eat the lemmings that her parents caught. It was the only food they could find. Her mother cried. Her father threatened. But Lusa wouldn't budge. "I don't like birds and I won't eat birds and that's that."

Lusa's parents tried everything to get her to eat the lemmings. They took the bones out. They mixed the bird meat with eggs. But Lusa wouldn't eat anything that had bird in it. Her parents finally had to give in and let her eat just the few eggs that they were able to find. They didn't know what else to do.

Now that Lusa is older, she is willing to eat certain birds, but only the biggest and fattest ones. Sometimes this means she goes hungry. But that is the choice Lusa has made and she has to live with it. All the other foxes just shake their heads. "That's one stubborn fox," they say. Lusa's stubbornness makes it very hard for her to keep her belly full.

Unlike her best friend, Amka, Lusa is always on the lookout for danger. Early one morning, the two young foxes go out to search for bird eggs. It's their favorite breakfast. But some bird's make their nests in very hard to reach places, like on the edge of rocky cliffs. This makes it tough for foxes or other animals to steal their eggs.

"Yesterday I found a big peregrine falcon nest," says Amka. "Let's go check and see if it has eggs in it this morning."

Lusa stops walking. "Is the nest easy to reach? I am not going to risk falling off the edge of a cliff, you know."

"I know," says Amka. "I think if we help each other, it won't be any trouble to reach the nest."

"No trouble? We'll see," says Lusa. She remembers the many times that Amka has said something was no trouble and it ended up being heaps of trouble. She will follow Amka and then make her decision once they reach the nest.

It takes them about a half an hour to get to the edge of the rocky cliff. Amka paces back and forth along the edge and finally shouts, "Aha! Here it is. And it has two eggs; one for you and one for me."

Lusa moves up beside her, peers over the edge, and shakes her head. "No way, it's too far down. We'll never reach it."

"Don't be so negative," says Amka. "I've reached nests that are way further than this before."

"And you have nearly died several times from falling off cliffs." Lusa refuses to help her friend. "Let's go look for a less dangerous breakfast," she says and walks off.

Amka looks at the eggs and looks at her friend who moves further and further away. With a huge sigh, she trots after Lusa and catches up with her. The two young foxes walk side by side, but don't say a word to one another.

Thankfully, they found a snack on the way. Soon their bellies are full and they find a spot in the meadow grass to rest. Amka shakes her head. "You really are the most stubborn fox of all," she says. "But I think maybe you were right about that nest. It was in a dangerous spot. Thanks for stopping me. Your stubbornness may have saved my life."

Lusa is surprised and smiles at her friend. "This is the first time anyone has ever thanked me for being stubborn," she says. "I always thought being stubborn was a bad thing."

Her friend Amka pokes at Lusa's ribs. "It can be a bad thing, especially if you get hungry from not eating. Or if you are being rude and disagreeable because of it, but being stubborn can keep you out of trouble sometimes, too. Being stubborn can be good when you direct it towards getting things done, or solving problems. Stubborn people don't quit, and that's a good thing."

Lusa thinks about what her friends says. From now on, she's going to try to use her stubbornness just for good things. And maybe, just maybe, she'll try to eat more birds.

Chapter Four

A pod of black and white killer whales, also known as orcas, fly through the icy cold arctic waters together. Their black dorsal fins are often seen sticking out above the water. When this happens, it's like a warning flag for the animals that can become the orcas next meal. Orcas are super fast swimmers and must work together as teams to hunt for seals. Squid, fish, and octopus also are part of their diet. Because they use up so much energy swimming, the orcas have to eat about 300 pounds of food every day. That's a lot of food!

Koko is one of twenty members of his pod, which is what a group of orcas are called. They spend most of their days hunting for food, but they have plenty of time to play, too. The young ones like to practice some of the tricks they use to hunt. Making big waves together is a favorite of the young members of the pod.

Making waves isn't easy. It takes at least three orcas swimming side by side for a couple hundred feet and then swishing their flukes as they dive under a small ice shelf. Flukes are whale tails. The whales can make big waves and splashes with their tails or flukes. The most important thing is that the orcas work together as a team. Koko and his two friends, Aput and Opik, have been swimming together as part of their pod since they were born. The three young whale calves were born just a few months apart. They always team up together when it's time for training or playtime. Aput is the bossiest of the group. Opik usually goes along with whatever Aput decides, but Koko doesn't always agree with Aput's plans.

"We need to practice making waves over ice sheets," says Opik. "Let's go find a big one."

"Why does it have to be a big one?" asks Koko. "Wouldn't it be better to practice on a smaller one?"

Opik shakes his head. "We aren't babies anymore. We need to train to be able to knock seals off the big ice sheets."

Aput listens as his two friends argue. He waits for them to finish, then he offers an idea. "Why don't we look for a medium-size ice sheet?"

Opik and Koko nod their heads in agreement. "Good idea."

So the three young orcas swim off together to find a medium-sized sheet of ice. But it isn't long before the arguing starts up again. Koko stops at an ice sheet. "This is about the right size," he says.

"No it isn't," says Opik. "It's too small. It won't be a challenge for us."

And so it goes for the next half an hour. Each time they find an ice sheet Koko thinks it's too big and Opik says it's too small. Aput is very patient with them, but he is getting tired. "Please listen," he says. "We are wasting way too much time searching and not enough time training." He points to an ice sheet. "I think that one will be just fine for what we need to do."

Opik and Koko are getting tired, so they agree to Aput's suggestion.

In order to make a wave wash over an ice sheet, the three whales need to line up side-by-side at a good distance from the ice sheet and swim really fast together. Right before they arrive at the ice sheet, they must swish their tail fins at the same time and then dive under the ice sheet. This causes a wave of water to cover the ice sheet and will knock into the ocean anything that is hanging out on the top of the ice.

The first time they try, Aput slows down and they don't reach the ice sheet at the same time. The second time, Opik swishes his tail fin too early which makes the wave too small. After two more failed attempts, the three of them are tired and getting crankier and crankier. "We must try again," says Opik. "We can't leave until we get this right."

"I'm leaving," says Koko. "I'm tired and hungry."

Aput sees the look in Opik's eyes and tries to convince Koko to try one more time. "We can do this. We're really close. Just once more."

Even though it's getting late, they swim out and line up to try again, but their timing is still off and they are not able to make a wave. Koko swims off towards the setting sun without saying a word to his two friends. Aput follows him, but Opik stays behind. He shouts out, "One more try. I know we can do this." But the other two keep swimming away. Opik hurries after them.

When he catches up he tries to speak to Koko, but his friend ignores him and keeps swimming. Koko is hungry and is searching for food. Opik thinks he spots a bunch of squid, but Koko argues with him. "That's just a shadow, not squid." Aput looks in the direction that Opik is pointing. "I think Opik is right. I think there might be squid over there." They argue back and forth for several minutes, but Koko doesn't believe them and swims off again towards the sunset. Aput yells after him, "Come on. Just try."

"Forget about him. Let's go eat those squid," says Opik. And so Aput and Opik swim off towards the shadow. But Koko is right. What they think is a squad of squid turns out to be just a shadow after all. Disappointed, they swim fast to catch up with Koko, but he is too far away from them already. When they reach the pod, they search for their friend and find him eating scraps from a seal that his big sister caught.

Koko nudges some of the scraps toward Aput and Opik. "You hungry?"

They accept the food with joy and gulp it down quickly. "You were right about the shadow," says Aput.

Koko makes a face at Opik. "I told you so."

Opik's anger flares up. "You think you're always right, but you're not," he says. "Remember the time I spotted that group of octopi and you didn't believe me and..."

The two of them start arguing again. Their voices get louder and louder. Aput tries to stop them, but they pay no attention to him. Some of the other orcas gather around to listen. The crowd grows. Then a loud voice shouts, "Enough of this!"

It's Koko's mother. "Listen up," she says and slaps her tail fin hard on the surface of the water to get their attention. Opik and Koko close their mouths immediately. Koko's mother continues.

"This pod has had enough of the two of you and your constant arguing. We are a family and this family requires teamwork to survive. Teams work together. Are the two of you part of this family, part of this team, or not?" she asks.

Koko and Opik tip their heads up and down. Koko's mother makes them feel nervous. They hate it when she's mad. They look at each other and then answer. "Yes, we are a team."

"Well then," says Koko's mother. "You need to start listening to each other. It doesn't matter who's right or who's wrong. What's important is that you respect each other's ideas and work together. If not, you will not survive. Do you think you can work together and stop arguing all the time?"

Aput swims in between his two friends. "I think they can."

Opik and Koko draw closer to Aput, thankful for his trust in them. "We will try."

"Make it happen," says Koko's mother. "I don't want to hear about anyone arguing or bickering anymore."

The entire group of young orcas, including Koko and Opik, bob up and down in agreement. "Yes, ma'am," they say. "No more arguing."

The next day, Koko, Opik, and Abut head out to practice making waves over a large ice sheet. On their second attempt, they are able to make a huge wave together. They clap their fins together and shout together. "We did it! Teamwork wins!"

Chapter Five

High up in the deep blue sky, one of the most beautiful arctic birds soars. The snowy owl spreads her white wings wide as she scans the ground looking for her brothers. Yura is mostly white, but she has brown bars and spots on her back and wings. Her brothers are almost all white and sometimes that makes it hard for her to spot them on the snowy ground.

She has been hunting hares and lemmings all day, but without any success. Her brothers are much better hunters. Sometimes they give her what's left of their food. She scans the grassy area where her oldest brother has his nest, but he's not there. So, she moves on to find her younger brother. From high in the sky, her excellent golden eyes spot him and he's eating something. Yura swoops down and lands beside him. "Hey! Give me something to eat. I'm starving," she says.

Her younger brother frowns. "Have you ever heard of the word 'please'?" he asks.

Yura shrugs. "Whatever. Sharing is caring. So if you care, you'll share with me," she says. "You know *those* words, right?"

The young owl doesn't answer, but he uses his claws to tear off a piece of meat and gives it to his big sister. She gulps it down. "Is that all you're gonna give me?" she asks. "You're being greedy." Her brother sighs and tears off another piece. She swallows it and looks around. "Where's our big brother? Has he caught anything today?"

"I haven't seen him lately."

Yura flaps her wings and is ready to take flight again. "See ya."

"Haven't you forgotten something?" her brother asks. But she's already gone. Her brother shakes his head and mutters to himself. "No please. No thank you. Next time I'm not sharing or caring. She can find her own food or starve."

Yura can't find her older brother, so she heads back to her own nest. It's in an open space on the ground where she can see in all directions and where she can watch out for foxes. As she approaches her nest, she spots a tasty snack and swoops down to grab it. She catches it on the first try. So easy!

Yura is just starting to eat when her chubby friend, Aluki, shows up. "I haven't eaten all day," she says. "You don't mind if I have a few bites, do you?"

Yura points to Aluki's belly. "I don't think it would hurt you to stop eating for a few days," she says. "You're getting bigger than the rest of us."

"Oh," Aluki says as she looks down at her belly. Her golden eyes well up with tears. No one has ever said that to her before. Feelings hurt; she flies off without another word. Even though Aluki is super hungry, she doesn't eat again for several days.

Not long after Aluki leaves, Yura's oldest brother lands beside her. "You catch that snack by yourself?" he asks.

"Sure did," she says, her voice full of pride. "First try."

"Good for you," her brother says. "It took me years to master that skill."

"Well," says Yura. "That's probably because you aren't able to make turns as fast as I can."

"What do you mean?" her brother asks. "What makes you think you fly better than me?"

Yura touches her right wing to his. "It's because of these feathers of yours. Haven't you ever noticed they're shorter than all the other snowy owls' wing feathers?"

Her older brother examines his wing feathers. "They're not shorter."

"Yes they are," Yura says. "Everyone talks about them. Hasn't anyone ever pointed this out to you?"

Yura's brother looks closely at his wing feathers. Maybe they do seem a little shorter. He used to be so proud of their pure white color. Now he sees them as something ugly. But what really bothers him is that it's his little sister who has pointed out the defect. Is it true that everyone talks about his short feathers behind his back? Why has no one ever mentioned it to him before? Why didn't his parents tell him?

Downhearted, Yura's brother takes flight. As he flaps his wings, he feels heavy and slow. The joy he used to feel when flying is gone. Later, he finds his mother in her nest and pours out his feelings to her. His mother assures him that there is nothing wrong with his wing feathers. She reminds him that they are just like his fathers. "And your father is known as one of the best flyers in the entire Arctic region!"

This cheers up her son and he flies away happy again.

As she watches him soar through the sky, Yura's mother thinks about what to do about Yura. Earlier, she was visited by her younger son and also Aluki's mother. They both talked about Yura and the hurtful things she'd been saying. Her mother flies off to find her.

Yura is sitting in her nest when her mother lands beside her. She can tell by the look on her mother's face that something serious has happened. "What's wrong?" she asks.

Her mother looks her up and down. "You've been acting mean and ungrateful. It's not okay to be rude and negative. Your words have the power to uplift or destroy others, and lately you've been destroying others with your hurtful comments. What if I told you that you are lazy and ugly and that no one wants to be your friend?"

Yura is shocked. Her mother has never spoken to her like this before. Her mouth quivers beneath her beak. She fights back tears. She doesn't know what to say.

Her mother's big golden eyes narrow. "How do those words make you feel?"

Yura bursts out crying. "They hurt my feelings. Why did you say those mean things to me?"

Yura's mother pretends to be surprised. "Words hurt feelings?"

"Yes they do." Yura sniffs.

Her mother puts a wing around her. "I want you to think about the words you've been using with your brothers and your friends, Yura. Do you think maybe your words have been hurting other people's feelings? Sometimes when we put others down we secretly hope we will feel better about ourselves. But it doesn't work. We will not truly feel better inside when we make others feel bad. It's only when we encourage and help others that we begin to feel better ourselves. Try it."

Yura thinks about what she's said to others lately. Maybe some of the things she's said have not been so nice. "But I didn't mean to hurt anyone's feelings," she says.

"Of course you didn't. Not on purpose," her mother says. "But I think you need to be more careful about how you choose your words. You need to think before your speak."

"Think about what?"

Her mother gives her a squeeze. "Think about how your words might make others feel before you say them."

Yura thinks about it for a minute. "I'll try. I really don't want to hurt anyone's feelings."

"That's great, my dear. It might be a good idea to go tell your brothers and Aluki that you're sorry."

Yura nods in agreement. "Good idea, Mother. I'll go right now."

Chapter Six

Harp seals live dangerous lives. They are hunted in the ocean by orcas. They are hunted on land by polar bears. They must always be careful everywhere they go. Becoming really good swimmers is a very important part of a young seal's life. When a baby harp seal is just eighteen days old, it starts to learn to swim by beating the water with its front flippers. Because of this, these young seals are called beaters.

Siluk is one of the first of the beaters to learn to swim because he is a bold and fearless young seal. He dives into the water without thinking about anything but filling his belly with fish, shrimp and crab and having fun. What he likes most of all is swimming in loops around his friends and making them laugh. He never worries. He is carefree and happy. But he is also careless.

Every morning his mother and father warn him to be careful. Siluk always smiles and waves his flipper, "No worries!"

The most dangerous time for harp seals is when they come up for air at an ice hole. That's one of the places the polar bears patiently wait to catch the seals. It's hard to know if there is a polar bear waiting or not. Most of the seals don't want to be the first to take a breath, but Siluk isn't afraid. Sometimes he races his friends to the ice hole. They always let him win since they don't want to be first. "Careful. Careful," they say.

Sometimes the seals get tired after swimming around for hours, so they search out a big sheet of ice to take a rest. The ice sheets are like little islands in the middle of the ocean. The bigger the better since orcas like to make waves over the ice sheets. If they make a big enough wave, the seals will fall into the water and that's very dangerous.

Siluk doesn't worry about falling into the water. When he is tired, he looks for the first ice sheet he can find. His friends are always warning him, "Be careful. Be careful."

But he always gives the same response. "No worries. I'll be fine."

This particular day has been especially fun since the young seals have found schools and schools of fish. They have eaten so much, all they want to do is find a place to rest and take naps. As usual, Siluk is not too concerned about resting on a big sheet of ice. Even though his friends beg him to come with them to find a safer place, he just shakes his head. "This place is good. Not an orca in sight."

His friends leave him. They feel scared for him, but there's nothing they can do.

Siluk spreads himself out in the middle of the small ice sheet and closes his eyes. But it isn't quite ten minutes later when he feels the ice sheet rocking a bit. He opens his eyes and gasps as he sees three black fins moving across the water. Orcas!

Too late to swim to safety, he clings to the ice and hopes that the killer whales haven't spotted him. A few minutes later, the first wave of water washes over the ice. Siluk shakes with fear. The waves come a second and third time, but somehow, he is able to keep from falling into the water. A few minutes later, the orcas are swimming off toward the sun. Though his heart is still pounding, Siluk heaves a huge sigh of relief.

He waits another half an hour before diving back into the water to head home. On the way, he has to swim under a huge ice sheet that is too big to pass under without coming up to a hole to take a breath. He is in a hurry to get home and doesn't think about the danger that may be waiting at the breathing hole. His nostrils rise above the water and as he takes a deep gulp of air, something scratches across his nose. He dives back down under the water. Something grabs hold of his back flippers. He struggles with all his might to break loose of the grip. Finally, he gets free and races towards home.

When Siluk pops up on the ice shelf where his friends and family are resting, they all gasp in horror and murmur. Siluk is shaking but he tries to pretend everything is okay. "No worries," he says. "I'm fine."

But he's not fine. His mother and father draw close and examine his body. He has a huge gash across his nose and part of one of his back flippers has been torn away.

"How did this happen?" his parents ask.

All of the other seals gather around to hear what Siluk has to say. He tells the story of getting away from the three orcas and then how he was attacked by a polar bear at the ice hole. The seals all shake their heads. "We are so glad that you are okay. You should be grateful that you are still alive," they say.

His mother and father give him comfort, but at the same time they know that his careless example must be used to help the other young seals.

They invite them to gather in a circle around their son. All of them take a good look at Siluk's wounds.

"This is what happens when seals are careless. All of you need to be extra careful when approaching breathing holes and everywhere else where there is danger."

The young seals nod in agreement. Siluk's parents ask him if he has anything he wants to say to his friends.

Siluk feels ashamed and is embarrassed to speak, but he does want to say something. "I know that most of you have told me many times to be more careful. I should have listened to you. I am glad that I am still alive. My hope is that we can all continue to help each other. I promise to be extra careful from now on."

His friends gather around him and show their support by patting him gently with their flippers.

Will You Help Us Out?

Would you please consider leaving reviews for our books? Reviews don't have to be long and will only take a minute. It would mean a lot and help us get the word out, to other children, as well. Thank you so much!

AFTERWORD

Thanks again for picking up this book! You are participating in making our world a better place to live and grow. When children learn that they will always get back what they give, they will start to navigate their lives in incredible ways. When you give a smile, and make someone's heart feel lighter and happier, because of it, you can be sure that you will receive something in the near future that will make your heart happier as well. When you do something kind for someone, you can be sure that someone will do something kind for you in the coming days ahead. It is truly amazing how it works! Have fun with it and enjoy!

For more of our *Karma for Kids Books* please visit us at:

www.karmaforkidsbooks.wordpress.com
or
www.findyourwaypublishing.com

Find Norma MacDonald and her books online at Amazon.com.

Kyle Kitten and Friends: Short Stories, Fuzzy Animals, and Life Lessons

The Panda Family Relies on Each Other: Short Stories, Fuzzy Animals, and Life Lessons

Matt the African Meerkat and Friends: Short Stories, Fuzzy Animals, and Life Lessons

The Many Adventures of Peppy the Emperor Penguin: Short Stories, Fuzzy Animals, and Life Lessons
Kimmie Koala and Friends: Short Stories, Fuzzy Animals, and Life Lessons

Cranky Crocodile Saves the Day: Short Stories, Fuzzy Animals, and Life Lessons

Lucy Llama and Friends: Short Stories, Fuzzy Animals, and Life Lessons

Ethan the Eagle and Friends; Short Stories, Fuzzy Animals, and Life Lessons

Billy Brown Bear and Friends; Short Stories, Fuzzy Animals, and Life Lessons

Humble Heron and Friends; Short Stories, Fuzzy Animals, and Life Lessons

Peter Penguin and Friends; Short Stories, Fuzzy Animals, and Life Lessons

Other books that we recommend to help children learn important life lessons:

Guaranteed Success for Kindergarten; 50 Easy Things You Can Do Today! by Marrae Kimball

Guaranteed Success for Grade School; 50 Easy Things You Can Do Today! by Marrae Kimball

The Secret Combination to Middle School: Real Advice from Real Kids, Ideas for Success, and Much More! by Marrae Kimball

↔

Again, thank you for reading and sharing this book! YOU are making the world a better place. Please consider leaving a short review as it helps us spread the message! Children deserve the very best that life offers. All children deserve a chance at a successful and happy life.

If you have ideas for stories, please feel free to share and send them to:

Melissa Eshleman
Find Your Way Publishing, Inc.
PO Box 667
Norway, ME 04268
Melissa@findyourwaypublishing.com

www.findyourwaypublishing.com

Thank you!

Disclaimer

The purpose of this book is for entertainment purposes only. This book is designed to provide information and motivation to our readers. The content of each story is the sole expression and opinion of its author, and not necessarily that of the publisher. Names, characters, businesses, places, and incidents are either the products of the authors' imaginations or used in a fictitious manner. Any resemblance to actual persons, living or dead, businesses, companies, events, locales, or actual events is entirely coincidental. This book is not intended nor is it implied to be a substitute for professional medical advice, and any medical advice and any medical information contained in this book is not intended to be diagnostic or treatment in any way. The author and publisher are not engaged in rendering medical, psychological, legal, or any other professional services. If medical, psychological or other expert assistance is required, please talk to your physician and locate the services of a competent professional. The author and publisher shall have neither liability nor responsibility to any person or entity with respect to any loss or damage caused, or alleged to have been caused, directly or indirectly, by the information contained in this book. Neither the publisher nor the individual author(s) shall be liable for any physical, psychological, emotional, financial, or commercial damages, including, but not limited to, special, incidental, consequential or other damages. If you do not wish to be bound by the above, you may return this book along with a copy of the receipt to the publisher for a full refund.